My hope is this exploration of these meanings
will bring a little Christmas memory in each of
the next twelve months.

Introduction

I was once told about the 12 Days of Christmas by my Mother on Christmas eve.

I was a young girl, still believing in Santa at the age of 10, wanting all of the magic of the season to be real.

But then one day in church I was told this version of the 12 Days Of Christmas.

Was it a secret version only to be said to the select few at mass?

This was not the version my mother told me on a Christmas Eve to calm me so I could sleep.

Many years have passed, and I found this version again, It is no secret; it is just not told very often,

Just a beautiful way to think of the glorious season of Christmas.

A wonderful Christmas day in your mind, in your heart.

On the First Day of Christmas,
my true love gave to me
A Partridge in a Pear Tree.

Symbolic of the baby Jesus arrival in the world.
The reason for the season, and a celebration
for 12 days to come!

On the Second day of Christmas,
my true love gave to me
Two Turtle Doves.

Symbolic of the New and the Old Testament.
Characteristic of love birds and companionship
You and your Beloved
Also, with your family and friends
This second day is a very strong day to make
plans for you and the world.
To be there with enthusiasm and energy
for those around you

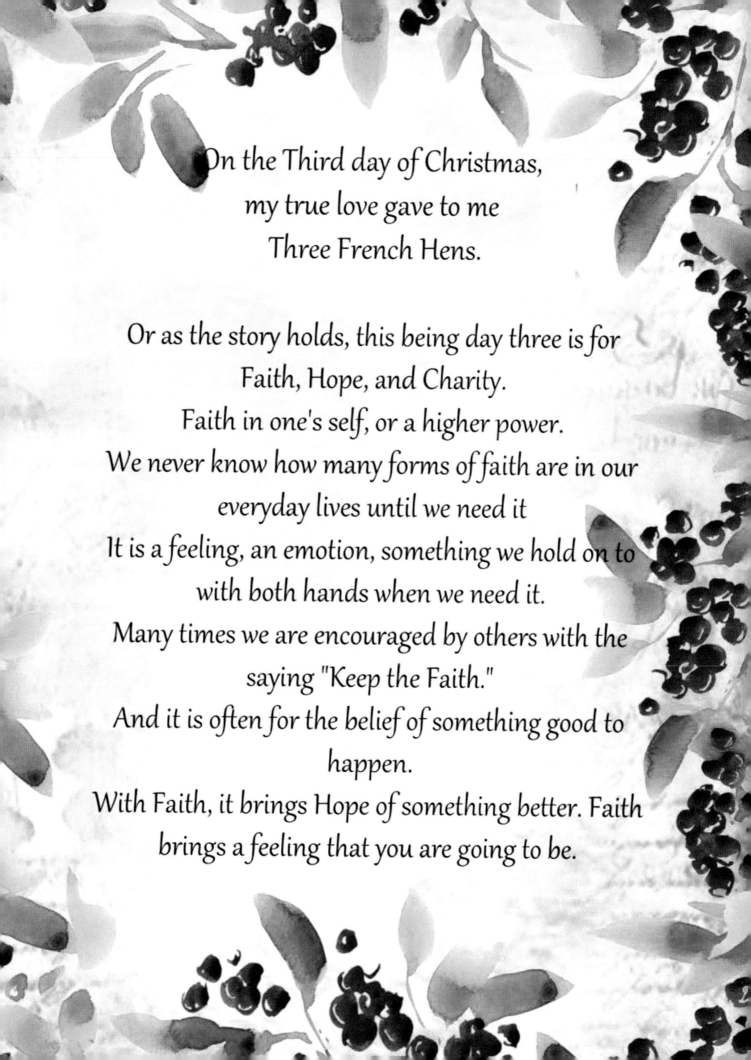

On the Third day of Christmas,
my true love gave to me
Three French Hens.

Or as the story holds, this being day three is for
Faith, Hope, and Charity.
Faith in one's self, or a higher power.
We never know how many forms of faith are in our
everyday lives until we need it
It is a feeling, an emotion, something we hold on to
with both hands when we need it.
Many times we are encouraged by others with the
saying "Keep the Faith."
And it is often for the belief of something good to
happen.
With Faith, it brings Hope of something better. Faith
brings a feeling that you are going to be.

And think of the charitable acts you receive or are witness to during this Christmas season.

You might think 'I can not afford anything at this time', or 'I don't do charity'.

Well, monetary means does not define the act of charity.

It can be time spent with one less fortunate, a kind word or gesture, a smile when greeting another.

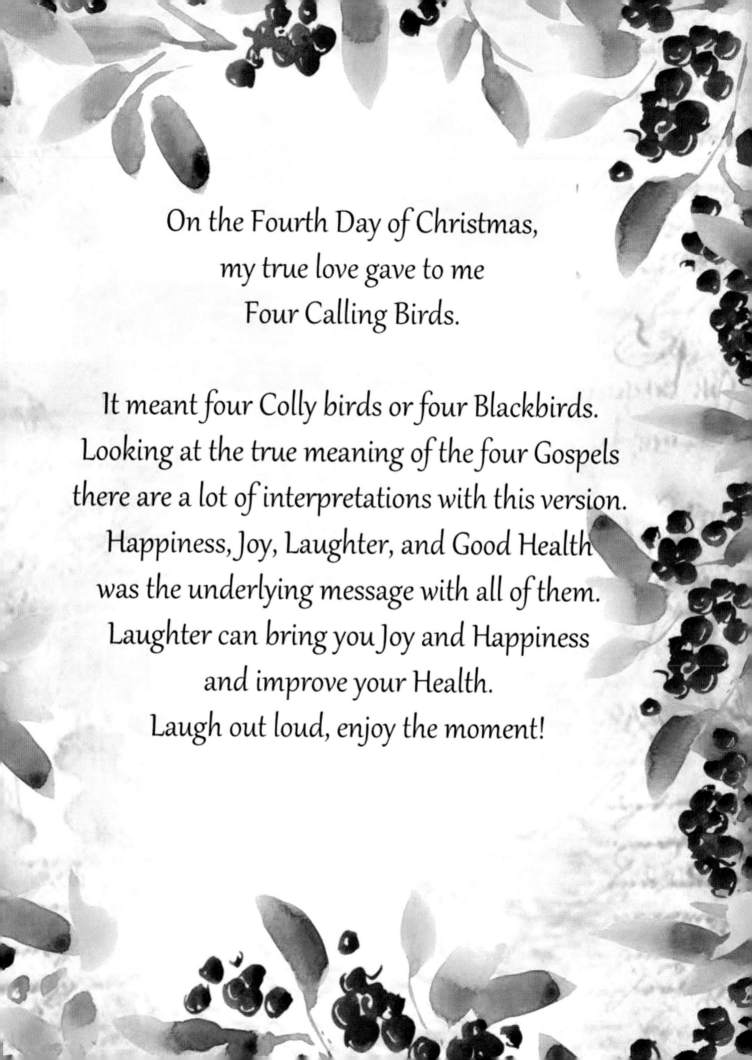

On the Fourth Day of Christmas,
my true love gave to me
Four Calling Birds.

It meant four Colly birds or four Blackbirds.
Looking at the true meaning of the four Gospels
there are a lot of interpretations with this version.
Happiness, Joy, Laughter, and Good Health
was the underlying message with all of them.
Laughter can bring you Joy and Happiness
and improve your Health.
Laugh out loud, enjoy the moment!

On the Fifth day of Christmas,
my true love gave to me
Five Golden Rings.

This line is shining a light on the five books
of the Old Testament.
So, we should be able to think of five
good things;
Five members of the family or friends
at your table.

On the Sixth day of Christmas,
my true love gave to me
Six Geese a Laying.

Symbolic of Creation.
The six days of creating the earth.
Think of the next six days
and what one can
create before Epiphany.
Think about what one can do in their
New Years Resolution.
The preparation to make things better!

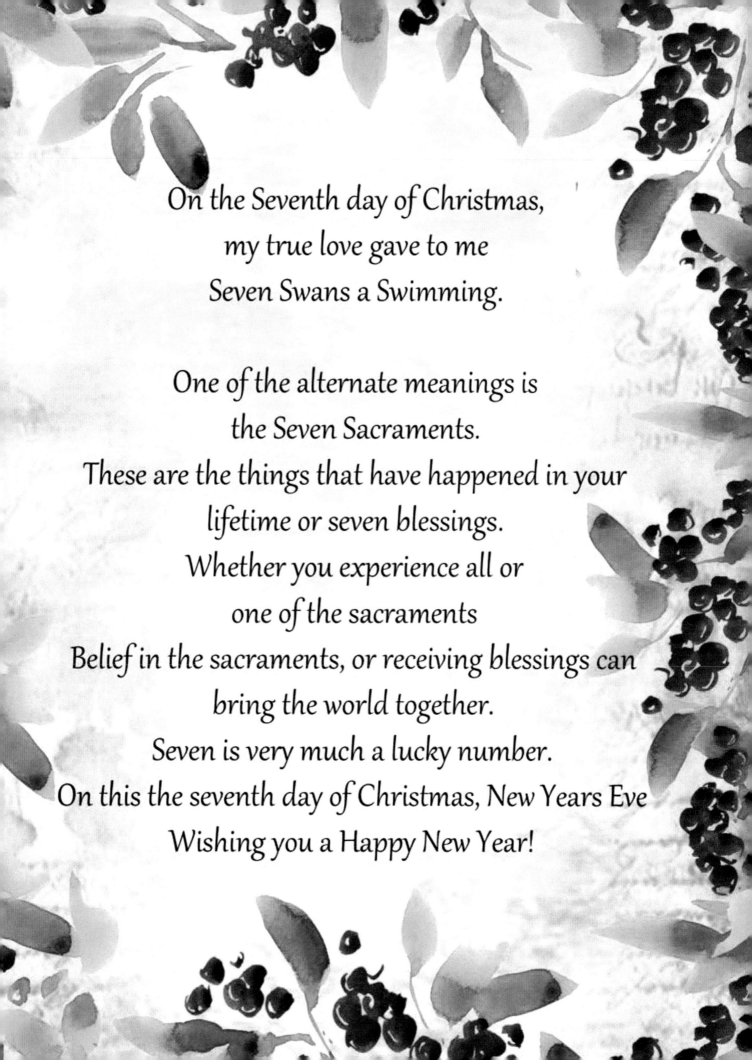

On the Seventh day of Christmas,
my true love gave to me
Seven Swans a Swimming.

One of the alternate meanings is
the Seven Sacraments.
These are the things that have happened in your
lifetime or seven blessings.
Whether you experience all or
one of the sacraments
Belief in the sacraments, or receiving blessings can
bring the world together.
Seven is very much a lucky number.
On this the seventh day of Christmas, New Years Eve
Wishing you a Happy New Year!

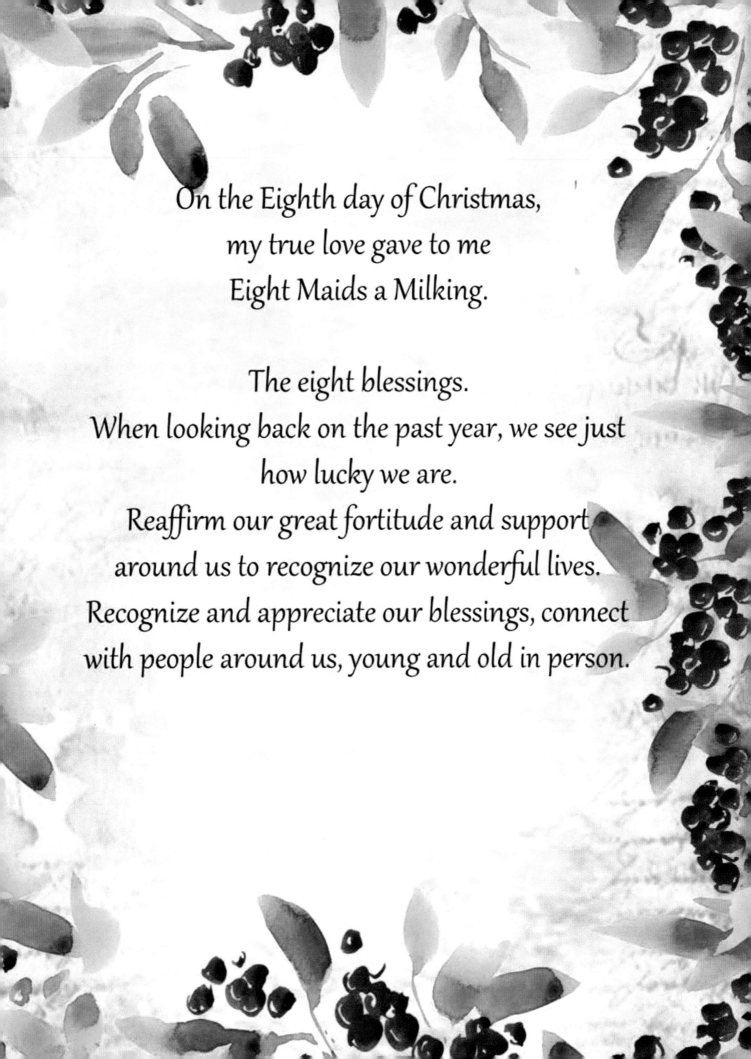

On the Eighth day of Christmas,
my true love gave to me
Eight Maids a Milking.

The eight blessings.
When looking back on the past year, we see just
how lucky we are.
Reaffirm our great fortitude and support
around us to recognize our wonderful lives.
Recognize and appreciate our blessings, connect
with people around us, young and old in person.

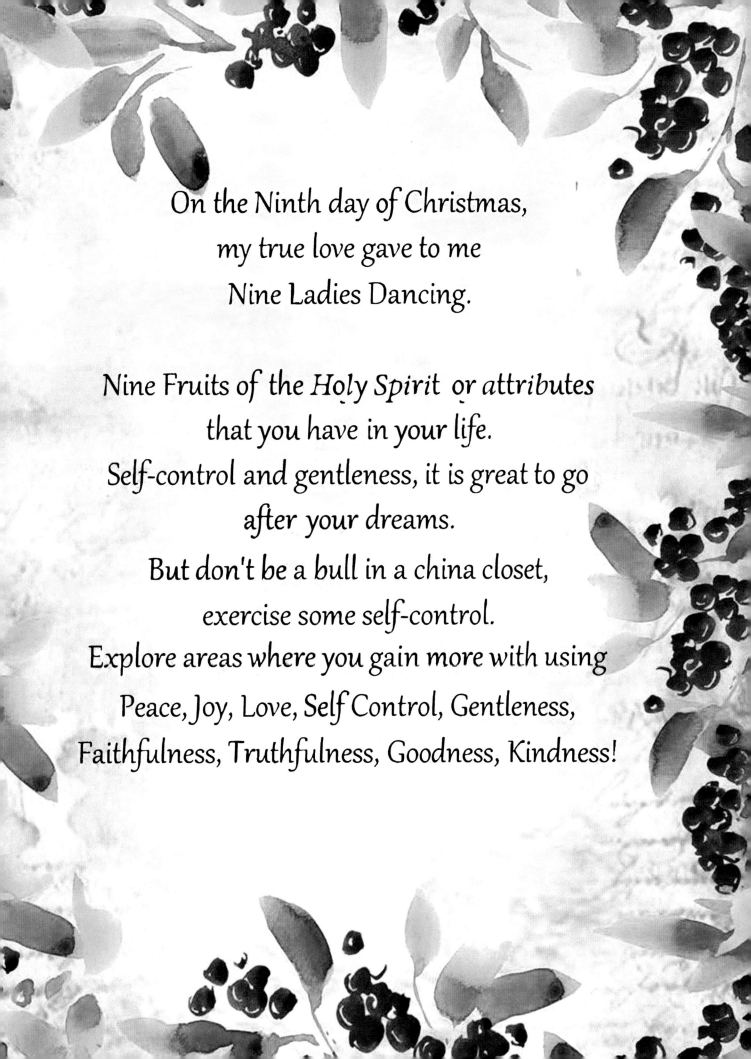

On the Ninth day of Christmas,
my true love gave to me
Nine Ladies Dancing.

Nine Fruits of the Holy Spirit or attributes
that you have in your life.
Self-control and gentleness, it is great to go
after your dreams.
But don't be a bull in a china closet,
exercise some self-control.
Explore areas where you gain more with using
Peace, Joy, Love, Self Control, Gentleness,
Faithfulness, Truthfulness, Goodness, Kindness!

On the Tenth day of Christmas,
my true love gave to me
Ten Lords a Leaping.

This is a reflection on the Ten Commandments
The ten things we should not do.
Focus on being a good person.
To thy own self be true, don't lie.
Think more of ten things you should do!

On the Eleventh day of Christmas,
my true love gave to me
Eleven Pipers Piping.

This is a reflection on the Eleven Apostles.
The Apostles without Judas.
Think of the friends that you have; cultivate more
friendships around you.
Let memories bring you peace.
Try and be the type of friend that others need.

On the Twelfth day of Christmas,
my true love gave to me
Twelve Drummers Drumming.

It is the 12 points of the Apostles Creed.
A passage that I know by memory.
Now when I recite it, I will remember
the Twelve Days Of Christmas.

EPIPHANY

Epiphany, commonly known as Three Kings' Day
or the Feast of the Epiphany.
Also known as 12th night, celebrating the three
wise men's visit to baby Jesus and also remembers
his baptism.

In literary terms, an epiphany begins with a
small, everyday occurrence or experience.
The coming six Sundays which follow Epiphany
are known as the time of manifestation.
Combine the 12 Days of Christmas and the
coming six Sundays to create a Happy New Year!

Made in the USA
Middletown, DE
05 September 2023

38048844R00018